Sparkle Fairies and the Imaginaries

To my Lolas
—G. S.

Daisy
DREAMER

#3

Sparkle Fairies and the Imaginaries

By Holly Anna • Illustrated by Genevieve Santos

LITTLE SIMON
New York London Toronto Sydney New Delhi

LITTLE SIMON

An imprint of Simon & Schuster Children's Publishing Division

1230 Avenue of the Americas, New York, New York 10020

First Little Simon hardcover edition August 2017

Copyright © 2017 by Simon & Schuster, Inc.

Also available in a Little Simon paperback edition.

All rights reserved, including the right of reproduction in whole or in part in any form.

LITTLE SIMON is a registered trademark of Simon & Schuster, Inc., and associated colophon is a trademark of Simon & Schuster, Inc. For information about special discounts for bulk purchases, please contact Simon & Schuster Special Sales at 1-866-506-1949 or business@simonandschuster.com. The Simon & Schuster Speakers Bureau can bring authors to your live event. For more information or to book an event contact the Simon & Schuster Speakers Bureau at 1-866-248-3049 or visit our website at www.simonspeakers.com.

Designed by Laura Roode

Manufactured in the United States of America 0617 FFG

2 4 6 8 10 9 7 5 3 1

Library of Congress Cataloging-in-Publication Data

Names: Anna, Holly, author. | Santos, Genevieve, illustrator.

Title: Sparkle Fairies and the Imaginaries / by Holly Anna ; illustrated by Genevieve Santos.

Description: First Little Simon paperback edition. | New York : Little Simon, 2017. | Series: Daisy Dreamer ; 3 | Summary: "Daisy Dreamer's totally true imaginary friend Posey invites her and her best friends Lily and Jasmine to the World of Make-Believe"— Provided by publisher.

Identifiers: LCCN 2016048170 | ISBN 9781481491853 (pbk) | ISBN 9781481491860 (hc) | ISBN 9781481491877 (eBook)

Subjects: | CYAC: Imagination—Fiction. | Imaginary playmates—Fiction. | Friendship—Fiction.

BISAC: JUVENILE FICTION / Imagination & Play. | JUVENILE FICTION / Humorous Stories. | JUVENILE FICTION / Readers / Chapter Books.

Classification: LCC PZ7.1.A568 Sp 2017 | DDC [Fic]—dc23

LC record available at https://lccn.loc.gov/2016048170

CONTENTS

CHAPTER ONE

Believe Me

Scritch-scratch!

Scritch-scratch!

I crawl through the starry-smooth tunnel to the Hideout—our secret meeting place under the slides at school. Jasmine and Lily scuff along behind me. Then we sit crisscross applesauce on the ground. I swish pebbles out from under me.

"The meeting of the Secret Journal Club is now called to order!" I say as I open my secret journal. It was a gift from my grandmother Upsy.

"What's on the agenda?" Lily asks, tossing her long dark hair over one shoulder.

I lean closer to my friends. "You'll never believe it," I begin.

Their eyes widen. "What?" they both say at the same time.

I check the tunnel to make sure no one's there.

"Remember my imaginary friend, Posey?" I ask.

Their heads bob up and down. Of course they remember Posey. It's not every day that an imaginary friend

appears out of thin air right in front of you.

"Well, he drew a *magic* door on my bedroom wall, and then we went to the WOM!" I say, sounding out each letter. *Double-U. Oh. Em.*

Lily and Jasmine make funny faces, because they have no idea about the WOM.

"WOM stands for the World of Make-Believe!" I say. *Obviously*.

This makes their eyebrows go way, way, *way* up.

"Are you saying the World of Make-Believe is a *real* place?" Jasmine asks.

I nod like crazy. "And it's beautiful! I got to bounce along a Rainbow Road and pick a raspberry-flavored flower. I also saw all kinds of magical creatures, like Moonsturs and Pretty Pixies! Posey and I even helped a

Cloud Critter unicorn named Andever find her melody!"

I can see I said a little too much, because Jasmine's and Lily's mouths are hanging open.

"Do you believe me?" I ask.

Then Lily swallows uncomfortably. "Sure, we believe you, Daisy. Don't we, Jasmine?"

But Lily can't fool me. I see her secretly poking Jasmine. I sigh loudly. "Okay, okay. I know it sounds a little far-fetched, but I promise it's all true. I even have *proof.*"

I reach inside the hidden pocket of my journal and pull out a letter. "Wa-la! This is the letter Posey wrote to me *after* I visited the WOM!"

Dear Daisy,
Thank you for visiting my world. Next time I'll introduce you to the Sparkle Fairies and the imaginaries. Did you know I'm an imaginary? I can't wait for our next ADVENTURE.
Love, POSEY

Hi!

Jasmine and Lily read the letter.

"You pinkie swear you didn't write this?" Lily says.

I hold out my pinkie finger. Lily hooks her pinkie onto mine. "Total pinkie swear!"

Then somebody giggles inside the tunnel. I whip my head around and peer down the passageway.

It's Gabby Gaburp and Carol Rattinger—my two worst enemies! As soon I look up, they do a mean chant,

"What's up Daisy Dreamer's sleeve? All she says is make-believe! Daisy Dreamer has no friends—so bluppity blup! She makes them up!"

Then my friends and I scramble to
our knees and chase those stinky girls
right out of the tunnel.

☆ Chapter Two ☆

Showtime!

After school I invite Jasmine and Lily over to my house. I have to prove to both of them that the World of Make-Believe is *real*. I mean, they are my best friends, and best friends share everything.

We bounce up the stairs like three springy springs. Then I tell them to sit on my bed and watch because it's *showtime*.

First I yank open my desk drawer, grab my purple marker, and pop off the cap. I walk to the wall and draw a door in three squeaks!

Squeeeeeeeeeeeeeak!

Squeeeeak!

Squeeeeeeeeeeeeeeeak!

"STOP!" Jasmine and Lily yell.

My friends are worried because I just drew on my wall. But I know there's nothing to worry about. *Obviously.* So I add a doorknob.

"It's erasable," I say, like no big whoop. Then I toss my marker back in the drawer.

"Now we're going to walk through this door on my wall and into the World of Make-Believe," I say. "I'll go first. Watch closely and do what I do."

My friends nod.

I walk to the drawing, reach for the doorknob, and *whomp!* I bang right into the wall.

"*Owie,*" I say, rubbing my forehead.

Jasmine and Lily giggle.

To say I'm slightly embarrassed would be slightly right. (Okay, totally right!)

"Why won't you work?" I ask the door. Then I grab at the knob again, but I can't get ahold of it because it's flat—like a drawing of a doorknob should be. I step back and scratch my head. Then there's a click, and the door swings open.

"Did somebody knock?" says a voice. It's Posey!

Now I'm a little annoyed. "No, I did *not* knock. I walked smack-dab into this drawing of a door I drew on my wall."

"Hmm. In the WOM we use our hands to knock on doors, not our faces!" Posey says with a chuckle. That's because he's a *big* chucklehead.

I roll my eyes and growl, "I was trying to walk through the door. *Obviously!*"

"Oh. There's a trick to that," he says. "But I'll show you later because you *and* your friends are needed in the WOM right away!"

When I turn around, Jasmine and Lily are sitting on my bed with their mouths hanging open—*again*.

"You heard him!" I say. "Let's go!"

☆ Chapter Three ☆

Trouble Ahead

Boing! Boing! Boing!

Jasmine, Lily, and I bounce along the Rainbow Road.

"So do you believe in the WOM now?" I ask. And, of course, they do. *Obviously.* Then I double-bounce Lily, and she flies up in the air and squeals.

Jasmine discovers a field of wild lollipop flowers. "May we pick them?"

"Um, okay," says Posey as he tries to keep inching us forward, "but we kind of need to keep moving!"

Why is Posey so antsy? I wonder. Then I shrug it off. I'm having too much fun looking at flowers with my friends to ask him why.

Jasmine picks a swirly orange marigold, and Lily chooses a cotton-candy tulip. I pick a daisy. *Obviously*. It has a bright lemon center and vanilla petals. Then we bounce onto the soft blue grass, flop onto our backs, and lick our lollipops.

"What are you doing now?" Posey asks. He claps his hands sharply. "We need to get going! *Chippity-chop!*"

"Look! Are those the Cloud Critters?" asks Lily.

Suddenly we're too busy watching clouds float by to pay attention to poor Posey. We spy a rabbit, a panda, a giraffe, and a kangaroo. Then I see my favorite Cloud Critter of all!

"Andever!" I shout to the unicorn cloud. I wave like crazy. Andever gives me a horn bob.

My friends both say, "Wowie wow," because now they actually believe me. Seeing is most definitely believing.

Then Posey yanks my arm.

"OW!" I yelp.

"Please, we have to *go!*" Posey says. "We've got trouble."

This makes the others sit up. "Trouble? What kind of trouble?"

Posey sighs heavily. "The trouble is between the Sparkle Fairies and the Imaginaries. They won't speak to each other."

Hmm, it sounds like there is a much longer story here. "Why not?" I ask.

And then Posey gives us our first World of Make-Believe history lesson. And, wowee-zowee, it's a doozy!

I'm a Believer

"Do you know how an imaginary friend comes to life?" Posey asks as we continue down the Rainbow Road.

We shake our heads because not even I'm totally sure how that all works.

"An imaginary friend comes to life when someone really *needs* or really *wants* them," Posey says. "It's magical."

Well, that makes sense because when I met Posey, it was magical. It happened right after I drew a picture of him in my journal.

Then I stop—right in the middle of Rainbow Road. "Wait, did my drawing somehow bring you to life?"

Posey has a twinkle in his eye.

"Exactly. I've always existed in the WOM, but I was invisible until you drew a picture of me. Now here I am."

That. Is. So. Cool, I think as we start walking again. "So my drawing actually brought us together?"

Posey puts his arm around my shoulders. "That, plus you can believe in imaginary things."

I whistle in amazement, because I am definitely a believer in imaginary things. *Obviously.*

"What about me?" Jasmine asks. "Do I have an imaginary friend?"

Posey removes his arm from my shoulder. "Of course you do!"

Jasmine grabs the air with her fist and pulls it back. "Yes!"

"Does that mean I have one too?" Lily asks.

This time Posey doesn't answer as quickly. "Well, yes, but that's exactly why we need your help. Your imaginary friend is a Sparkle Fairy."

Lily clasps her hands together. "I *love* fairies. I doodle them *all* the time!"

Posey nods. "That's why your imaginary friend is a Sparkle Fairy, but that is the problem. You see, the Imaginaries and the Sparkle Fairies are . . . hmm, what's the word . . . ah, yes—enemies."

"Enemies!" I gasp. How can they be enemies? This is the WOM, after all, where even the Golly Ghosts are friendly!

"It all goes back to the very first imaginary friend," he explains as we walk. "Her name was Sweetheart, and she was a Sparkle Fairy."

"Aw," Lily says sweetly. "That's such a cute name."

"It is," says Posey. "She was named by a little girl who drew a fairy and brought Sweetheart into the Real World. But when Sweetheart appeared, the girl was frightened. She told Sweetheart that the fairy wasn't real. The girl didn't believe in her own imaginary friend!"

We each whimper because that is as sad as sad gets.

"Now I see why believing is so important," I say.

Posey nods. "The little girl didn't mean to, but she broke Sweetheart's heart. Then other imaginary friends began to find homes, and Sweetheart felt all alone."

"So what happened?" I ask.

Posey's face falls as he answers me. "Sweetheart came back here to look for other fairies like her. She could not find any, so she decided to create her own imaginary friends . . . the Sparkle Fairies."

Lily sighs dreamily. "That sounds so magical."

Then Posey stops next to a large sign. "Not really," he says sadly. "Sweetheart was so angry at the happy Imaginaries that she turned the Sparkle Fairies against them. The two groups have never gotten along. Lily, since your imaginary friend is an Imaginary, the other fairies won't play with her. And the Imaginaries are scared to be her friend because she's also a Sparkle Fairy."

Lily suddenly claps her cheeks in alarm. "Oh no! Where is she now?"

Posey points to the sign above us. It points to the Kingdom of the Imaginaries.

Lily takes off running.

"Hey, what are you doing?" Posey asks.

"We have to find my fairy and help her!" Lily cheers.

And we know she's right, so we all chase after her.

KINGDOM
of the
Imaginaries

KitCat

We come to an arch made of shimmering rainbow bricks. Across the front it says KINGDOM OF THE IMAGINARIES. And below it, A FRIEND FOR EVERYONE. A wall stretches around the entire kingdom. Posey pushes a button, and the double doors open wide.

Jasmine, Lily, and I stare in wonder at the kingdom within.

"Magnificent!" I declare.

"Magical!" chimes in Jasmine.

In the middle of the kingdom stands a gingerbread castle—just like in a fairy tale. The top of each turret looks like a swirl of strawberry ice cream.

"Delicious!" Lily chimes in.

"Don't try to eat the buildings," Posey warns us. "The castle isn't really made of sweets—it just looks that way."

Inside, the city looks like a giant playground with swings, slides, zip lines, and hammocks. There are paths everywhere, and instead of buses or

cars, they have amusement park rides to get around. And the rides look like desserts! Twirling cupcakes, swinging banana splits, and spinning coconut-cream pies zip around the streets.

Imaginaries are everywhere, busy at work and play. They each look different. Some have horns, and some

have pom-poms—others have antlers like Posey. They come in all patterns, too. I see polka dots, stripes, solids, checks, plaids, and even paisleys.

Lots of Imaginaries look like stuffed animals—puppy dogs, bunnies, lions, koalas, and bears—anything you can imagine! *Obviously.*

As we skip across a peppermint-striped bridge, Jasmine bumps into a lion by accident. Then Jasmine squeals, "KitCat?"

I. Cannot. Believe it. Because, oh, I have seen this beautiful lion with the fluffy mane, pom-pom tail, and round green eyes before. "That's your old stuffed animal, Jasmine!"

She touches the lion and says, "You're *real*! But how is it possible? I thought I lost you."

"Nothing's ever lost in the World of Make-Believe," KitCat tells Jasmine. "It's just waiting to be found."

"Jasmine used to take KitCat *every-where*," I tell Posey.

KitCat swishes his pom-pom tail. "Until I fell out of the car at the gas station."

Jasmine gives KitCat the biggest person and stuffed-animal lion hug maybe ever. "You *poor* thing!" she cries. "I looked and looked and looked for you. I missed you so much!"

KitCat gasps for air, and Jasmine loosens her grip. "I missed you too," he says, catching his breath. "Now we're together again! Hey, remember when you hurled me onto the roof and I got stuck?"

Jasmine bursts out laughing. "I had to knock you down with a Frisbee! And that Frisbee is *still* on the roof!"

KitCat shakes his head. "Why did you throw me up there in the first place?"

Jasmine shrugs. "I wanted to see if you could fly."

Then KitCat leaps into the air and flies in a circle. "How's this for flying?" he says, and he whisks Jasmine upward as they fly in a loop way over our heads.

Lily taps Posey's shoulder like a woodpecker. "When can I meet *my* imaginary friend?"

Posey gently grabs hold of Lily's finger-pecking hand. "That's right. I almost forgot. Is *now* a good time?"

Chapter Six

Estrella

Our shoes rumble over the open draw-
bridge and into the colorful castle hall.
The queen of the Imaginaries sits high
on a heart-shaped throne. Swirling
staircases lead to the floor from either
side of her throne. Above the queen are
stained glass windows with pictures of
all the creatures from the WOM.

The queen stands when we enter.

She wears a pink fairy-tale dress, and a crown of jewels sits between her pointy, catlike ears. She holds a bejeweled scepter in her hand. Then— *tap, tap, tap*—she walks down a set of curvy stairs.

As she rounds the fountain in the middle of the hall, we see a young fairy girl leaning against the fountain's edge. The fairy is crying. The queen glances at the fairy as she continues in our direction. Then the queen stops right in front of Posey.

"Is this the child?" the queen asks, looking at Lily.

Posey bows. "Yes, Your Majesty."

Lily steps awkwardly before the queen and bows, because that's how you say hello to queens. *Obviously.*

"Does this fairy belong with you?" the queen asks.

Then Lily does another super-quick curtsy, because she's not sure what else to do. "I hope so, Your Majesty!"

The queen lifts her staff toward the fairy. "Then go to her."

Lily nods and walks carefully to

the fairy's side. We gather round.

"My name is Lily," she whisper-tells the Sparkle Fairy Imaginary. "And I've been looking for you my *whole* life."

The fairy sits up and wipes the tears from her eyes. Then Lily opens her arms wide, and they hug. Happy sighs fill the hall.

"What's your name?" Lily asks.

The fairy gently brushes a lock of dark hair from her eyes. "I do not have one," she says. "The Sparkle Fairies won't give me a name."

Lily throws her head back in surprise. "Then I will!" she declares. "Your name will be . . . Estrella. That is Spanish for 'star,' and you are a star come to life!"

Posey and I share a look.

I give Lily a thumbs-up because she has given Estrella the perfect name.

Lily smiles back at me. Then she turns to the queen and asks, "Can we visit the Sparkle Fairies? We have to end this rotten feud once and for all."

I raise my hand as high as I can because I have a question that's been on my mind for a while. "Also, do you think we can fly this time? Or is KitCat the only one who flies?"

"*All* Imaginaries can fly," Posey says with a laugh. "All you had to do was ask!"

☆ Chapter Seven

The Same Old Story

Flying is not only for the birds anymore. I am riding on a cloud, just like it's my very own skateboard. Only, the road is a mile beneath me! I want to scream "WOW!" but I keep my mouth closed. I do *not* want to swallow any bugs. Yuck. No, thank you.

The WOM looks like a colorful patchwork quilt from high up in the sky. The mountaintops ahead of us shimmer and twinkle like the tiny points of a diamond.

"That's the Kingdom of the Sparkle Fairies," Posey says. "Shade your eyes as we get closer. Everything in this kingdom sparkles—*a lot.*"

Posey's right! The whole country-side shines—the valleys, the trees, the streams, and the flowers. I squint my eyes at first. Then I have to shade them from the brightness.

"Don't worry," Posey tells us. "Your eyes will adjust in a few minutes."

By the time we land, our eyes feel

better. We're standing in a field of glittering flowers. A waterfall tumbles with sparkling water. Atop the water-fall is a castle, and from the center of it all, the Sparkle Fairy queen flies down to greet us.

She is definitely the most beautiful Imaginary Friend I've ever seen—and believe me, I've seen a lot lately. She wears a fancy white gown covered in pearls that shimmer with rainbow light. Her long yellow curls fall around her wings, which match her gown.

We bow as she lands. When I stand up, I notice the Sparkle Fairies are almost the same size as we are—not teeny-tiny like the Pretty Pixies.

"Welcome," the queen says. "My name is Sweetheart. How may I help you?" She only addresses Jasmine, Lily, and me. She pays no attention to our imaginary friends.

Lily steps forward. "Your Majesty, we've come to mend the rift between the Imaginaries and the Sparkle Fairies."

Sweetheart shakes her head. "I am sorry, child, but I cannot grant your

request. Do you know the history of the Imaginaries and the Sparkle Fairies?"

Lily nods. "Posey told us all about it."

Sweetheart leans forward. "Well, now you will hear *my* side of the story."

At first her story is very similar to Posey's version. Except when Sweetheart tells it, we can hear her sadness about the little girl who didn't believe in her. Poor Sparkle Fairy! *Nobody* likes to feel left out.

When she finishes, Sweetheart pauses, and then she asks, "Do you know what we make here? Sparkle Fairies are the dream weavers of the Real World. We build dreams for every girl and boy in hopes that they will never lose their sense of imagination."

"Well, I daydream *all* the time!" I say, because it's true, I do. Sometimes I think that's why my name is Daisy Dreamer. "On the way over here I dreamed I had a slide from my bedroom window into my very own swimming pool."

"Oooooooh!" coo Jasmine and Lily.

"Sometimes I daydream about being a movie star," Lily says. "Or a talk-show host."

Jasmine and I pretend to primp our hair like glamorous movie stars.

Sweetheart watches us pretend and smiles. "All those dreams are built right here in my kingdom. Dreams let us believe we can do anything!"

That makes a lightbulb go on in my head. "Can you build a dream of getting along with the Imaginaries?"

My big idea surprises Sweetheart, and the happy expression drains right off her face. "No. I am sorry. I cannot build a dream like that."

Then, in a swirl of sparkles, the queen disappears.

Hmm. Maybe I should have said "Your Majesty."

Chapter Eight

A Friend

We fly all the way up to the Sparkle Fairy castle. There's no way we are going to give up *that easily. Obviously.*

KitCat grabs the brass handle on the castle door and pulls. The door doesn't budge. I know a thing or two about doors that won't open.

Posey flies to the queen's window, raps on the pane, and calls to her.

"Please, Your Majesty. We can work this out!"

Jasmine, Lily, and I rap the door knocker. "Please come out!" we beg.

Finally, Posey lands beside us. "Maybe Sweetheart needs time to calm down."

That makes sense. Upsy always says people need quiet time when they're upset.

But Lily disagrees. "Sweetheart's never going to calm down. She's been holding this grudge for too long."

Hmm, that makes sense too, I think,

gnawing the back of my thumb. *I wonder what in the world would heal Sweetheart's grudge against the Imaginaries?* Suddenly I stop gnawing.

"A *friend*," I say out loud. "All Sweetheart needs is a Real World friend!"

Jasmine and Lily look at each other and then back at me.

"But how are we going to do that?" asks Jasmine.

I smile mischievously and pretend to wave a magical wand. "Posey, can you please get us back to my room, double-quick! We need supplies."

Posey smiles. "No problem." Then he waves his hand *whoosh*, and away we swirl.

In no time we're back in my bedroom! I tell everyone my plan, and
we gather the supplies. Then I call out
each item on our super-special list to
make sure we have everything.

"Telephone?"

Nobody answers.

"Telephone?" I repeat.

"Wait, what's a telephone again?" Posey asks.

I point to the home phone I put in front of him and repeat my question.

"Telephone?"

"Check!" Posey says. Then he rubs the phone in his armpit, like a bar of soap. Ugh. It's a good thing he's not making the phone call.

"Letter?"

"Check!" says Estrella, holding the letter so everyone can see it.

"Erasable marker?"

"Yes! Here! I mean, check!" KitCat says. He has written all over his body.

"That's a regular marker," I say,

shaking my head. "Erasable marker?"

Jasmine holds up the right one this time. "Check!"

"Envelope?"

"Check!" Lily says, handing me an envelope.

Then I write an address on it.

Estrella hands me the letter, and I stuff it into the envelope and give it to Posey. "You know what to do—right?"

Posey nods.

"Remember," I tell him, "once you get to the house, you only have five minutes."

Posey salutes and flies out my window. Operation: Real-World Friend is a go.

☆ Chapter Nine ☆

Special Delivery!

I dial my grandmother.

"Hello?"

"Hi, Upsy!" I say into the receiver. "Did you get my special delivery in the mail today?"

I know this makes Upsy smile. "Why, I haven't checked my mailbox today. I'll go and do it right now."

I stay on the phone and listen as she

walks to the mailbox. I hope Posey got the letter there in time. He probably had to introduce himself to the mailbox. Then he most likely opened and closed it ten times. I'm sure he fiddled with the red flag too.

"I'm going down the front walk," Upsy says.

I hear the front gate creak.

"I'm opening the gate!" she tells me, and I hear the gate clink shut behind her. "I'm at the mailbox!"

The mailbox squeaks open, and Upsy says, "Oh, look, there's a letter in here from *you*. Imagine that!"

I jump in the air. Posey did it!

"Open it!" I cry.

"Wait till I get inside," Upsy says, and I can almost hear her smile. Then I listen as she shuts the mailbox and heads back through the gate and up the walk, crosses the porch, and opens the door to her house.

Finally she says, "Okay, I'm sitting at my desk with my letter opener!"

Sharrrip! She removes the letter and reads it out loud.

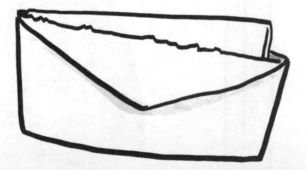

"'Dear Upsy, I love the journal you gave me so much. I especially like the story starters. I've had so much fun with them! Now I have a story starter for you! *There once was a magical friend named Sweetheart. . . .*'

"What a wonderful story starter, Daisy!" Upsy exclaims. "I also see a dot-to-dot on the back. I *love* dot-to-dots. Shall I do it now?"

I hold the phone out in front of me. "Yes!" I cry. "Do it *right* now!"

Upsy sets down the phone and con-
nects the dots. I can hardly wait for
her to be done.

"It's a fairy!" Upsy says. "A fairy named Sweetheart! Oh, I love her, Daisy. Thank you!"

"That's right! Well, I have to go, but I love you, and please enjoy your new imaginary Sparkle Fairy best friend ever bye-bye," I say in one quick breath. Then I hang up because we need to see if the plan worked.

CHAPTER TEN

Connecting the Dots

The door to the Sparkle Fairy castle is open this time. A warm, shimmering glow streams through the windows. Imaginaries flock through the gates into the castle, and the Sparkle fairies welcome them.

"It worked!" I cry. And I know it's true, because when Upsy connected the dots, she created an image of

Sweetheart. And the moment she com-
pleted the picture, Upsy and Sweetheart
became real imaginary friends—just
like Posey and me.

I grab Jasmine's and Lily's hands, and we dance around in a circle. Then we look for Sweetheart, but she finds us first.

"You've unlocked my heart!" she cries. "Someone believes in me! How did you do it?"

I blush. "I just helped connect a few dots."

"I feel happy and free!" Sweetheart exclaims. "I'll never allow myself to get hard-hearted again."

Then she takes Estrella's hands in hers. "I'm sorry for the way I treated you, Estrella. Please forgive me."

The two fairies smile and hug, making a swoosh of rainbow sparkles around them. It's the brightest bright ever!

Next Sweetheart calls to the entire room. "Hear ye! Hear ye! From this day forward, the Sparkle Fairies will

treat everyone with love, friendship, and respect."

Cheers fill the castle. I give my cheer an extra hoot because seeing everyone so happy fills my heart up so full I can't contain myself.

"Now let's celebrate!" Sweetheart cries as she waves her glittery scepter, and *kaboom!* A cannon explodes, and twinkling confetti showers down on everyone. We suddenly and magically have on sparkly party hats. There are cupcake towers everywhere, and the fountain in the middle of the room bubbles with strawberry lemonade.

"Now we *each* have imaginary friends!" I shout, and I pull Jasmine, Lily, Posey, KitCat, and Estrella into a great big group hug.

Then, from somewhere far, far away, I hear my name being called.

"Hold on!" I tell Lily and Jasmine. Then we swirl and swirl until we land safely on my bedroom floor once more. There's a knock on my bedroom door, and it swings open.

"I can call your parents if you girls would like to stay for dinner?" my mom asks, as if everything were a perfectly normal day.

"Sure!" Jasmine and Lily say, as if we've been in my bedroom for the whole afternoon.

Then my mom points to a ray of sunshine streaming through my bedroom window. The dust sparkles in the light.

"Pixies!" Mom exclaims. "Did you girls know Upsy used to tell me that the glittery dust in shafts of sunlight were pixies? What an imagination she has."

I share a surprised look with my friends, because hmm, maybe Upsy knows more about the World of Make-Believe than we thought.

Check out Daisy Dreamer's next adventure!

Clickety-clackety-clickety-clack!

I zoom down the sidewalk on my skateboard. The wind makes my hair fly out of my pigtails, and I have to spit it out of my mouth. *Pfffffffttt!*

"Hurry up, Mom!"

Mom and I are going to school *like always*, and I tease her *like always* because she is a slowpoke. Mom is walking and I'm on my skateboard, so I am wayyyyy in front of her. *Obviously!*

Suddenly a blast of light flashes in my eyes and blinds me! I can't see anything!

"Aaaaaaaaaaaaaaah!"

Then—*ka-bonkity bonk!*—I fall feet-over-helmet onto the sidewalk. WIPEOUT!!!

I hear footsteps rush to my side.

"Wow!" a girl says. "Are you okay?"

"Here, let us help you!" says another.

I look up and can't believe it! It's that awful Gabby Gaburp and her meanie sidekick, Carol Rattinger. What are *they* doing here? And why are they being so *nice*?

They pull me up and help me dust off. I have dirt all over my knees and elbows, but I don't hurt anywhere. Phew! While I am dusting, I check to make sure they haven't put a PRANK ME sign on my backpack.

Nope—all clear!

Then I double-check my skateboard in case they did something bad to it. But nothing seems different.